Ellie the Bouncing Unicorn

Story by: Mary Beth McFann

Artwork by: David Harshman

AuthorHouse™
1663 Liberty Drive
Bloomington, IN 47403
www.authorhouse.com
Phone: 1 (800) 839-8640

Published by AuthorHouse 08/21/2018

ISBN: 978-1-5462-5654-0 (sc)
ISBN: 978-1-5462-5655-7 (e)

Print information available on the last page.

Any people depicted in stock imagery provided by Getty Images are models,
and such images are being used for illustrative purposes only.
Certain stock imagery © Getty Images.

This book is printed on acid-free paper.

authorHOUSE®

Ellie the Bouncing Unicorn

Mary Beth McFann

This book is for my niece, Ellie, who is an exuberant 2-yr-old, full of life, loves unicorns, and LOVES jumping on her trampoline. Aunt Mary loves you very much, sweet girl, and I can't wait to see the amazing woman and person you become.

Love,

Aunt Mary

Ellie is a unicorn. She loves to dance and sing.

But there is one thing she loves more - it's bouncing, bouncing, bouncing!

Every day, she wakes up, and she rushes down the stairs...

She climbs onto her trampoline. She bounces without a care!

Now, unicorns can eat a lot, but her favorite thing to eat...

Is orange-flavored popsicles...so cold they make her squeak!

All that bouncing makes her sleepy, and so she takes a nap.

And when she wakes she is so hungry she
eats a unicorn snack!

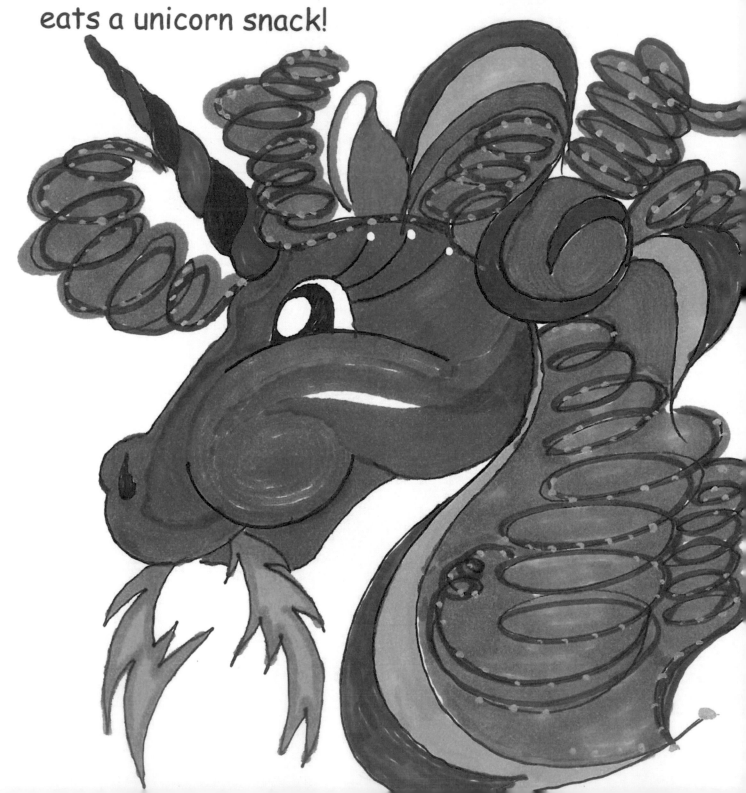

When snack time is over, Ellie prances off again...

Her trampoline is waiting, and her time is growing thin...

Now nighttime is approaching; Ellie soon will go to sleep.

And even in her dreams there are fluffy, bouncing sheep.

So make the most of your day, Ellie, there is bouncing left to do.

Ellie the Bouncing Unicorn – she bounces just like you!

Mary Beth McFann is a published poet, published songwriter, and children's book author. The inspiration for "Ellie the Bouncing Unicorn" came from her two-and-a-half year old niece, Ellie, who loves her trampoline and unicorns. This is Mary Beth's first children's book.

Printed in the United States
By Bookmasters